# Bamboo & Friends
# The Mushroom Ring

by Felicia Law
illustrated by Claire Philpott,
Karen Radford, and Xact Studio

Editor: Jill Kalz
Page Production: Brandie E. Shoemaker
Creative Director: Keith Griffin
Editorial Director: Carol Jones

First American edition published in 2007 by
Picture Window Books
5115 Excelsior Boulevard
Suite 232
Minneapolis, MN 55416
877-845-8392
www.picturewindowbooks.com

Printed in the United States of America.

**Library of Congress Cataloging-in-Publication Data**
Law, Felicia.
The mushroom ring / by Felicia Law ; illustrated by Claire
Philpott, Karen Radford, and Xact Studio.—1st American ed.
p. cm. — (Bamboo & friends)
Summary: Three animal friends in the rain forest wonder if
fairies are real and if mushrooms are really fairy rings.
ISBN-13: 978-1-4048-2595-6 (hardcover)
ISBN-10: 1-4048-2595-9 (hardcover)
[1. Mushrooms—Fiction. 2. Rain forest animals—Fiction.]
I. Philpott, Claire, ill. II. Radford, Karen, ill. III. Xact (Firm :
Delhi, India) IV. Title.
PZ7.L41835Mu 2007
[E]—dc22                                        2006003413

Bamboo, Velvet, and Beak sit on their log in the middle of the magical forest, just as they always do.

3

"I had a dream about fairies last night," says Bamboo.

4

"That's nice," says Velvet.
"Fairies are sparkly and sweet."

"They're not real," snaps Beak.
"They're make-believe."

"My fairies looked real enough," says Bamboo. "They were flying around, looking for mushrooms."

"Mushrooms?" cries Beak.
"Fairies don't eat mushrooms."

People eat lots of different kinds of mushrooms. But you should never eat a mushroom unless you know what kind it is. Some mushrooms are poisonous.

9

"They live inside rings of mushrooms called fairy rings," says Velvet. "They plant the mushrooms in circles and fly in and out, waving their magic wands and doing magic fairy things."

"You're teasing me, aren't you?"
asks Beak. "There are no such things
as fairies or fairy mushrooms."

"Look!" says Velvet, pointing across the clearing. "See that circle of mushrooms? That's a fairy ring!"

Some fairy rings are so large that they can be seen from airplanes in the sky.

13

Velvet is right. A perfectly formed
ring of tiny mushrooms is growing right
there in front of them.

"The fairies did that?" gasps Bamboo.

"It's called a fairy ring, but it wasn't made by fairies," says Beak. "You two need a nature lesson.

"Look here. See all of those pockets spreading out from the middle of the mushroom? They hold tiny seeds called spores.

A mushroom is the part of a fungus that sticks out of the ground. A fungus is a special form of life. It's not an animal or a plant.

17

"When the mushroom gets old, it pops open and ... POOF! All of the spores shoot out and float up into the air. Then they land in a circle and start to grow in a ring," Beak says.

Some mushroom spores can lie dormant, or go to sleep, for many years. Then they begin to grow again.

"See? No fairies!"

19

"Nature lessons!" says Velvet, shaking her head. "They're so puzzling."

"I like the fairy story better," agrees Bamboo. "It's easier to understand."

# Fun Facts

- Folk tales say that fairies don't like to be seen. They also don't like to have their names spoken. Some fairies are beautiful, while others are ugly.

- People in Scotland tell stories of ugly water fairies called gwyllions. Gwyllions try to make travelers lose their way at night.

- The dullahan is an Irish fairy. Stories say that the dullahan carries its head in its right hand and lifts it high to see many miles away.

- White truffles are the most costly kind of mushroom in the world. They grow mostly in Italy. People use trained pigs or dogs to sniff them out of the ground.

- *Fungi* is the word for more than one fungus. Mildew, molds, and mushrooms are kinds of fungi.

- Fungi feed on living or dead material. They spread out tiny threads over their food and then suck out the goodness.

## On the Web

FactHound offers a safe, fun way to find Internet sites related to this book. All of the sites on FactHound have been researched by our staff.

1. Visit *www.facthound.com*
2. Type in this special code for age-appropriate sites: 1404825959
3. Click on the FETCH IT button.

Your trusty FactHound will fetch the best sites for you!

## Look for all of the books in the Bamboo & Friends series: